Hellhound's Delight

JC Ballard

Published by JC Ballard, 2023.

This is a work of fiction. Similarities to real people, places, or events are entirely coincidental.

HELLHOUND'S DELIGHT

First edition. October 31, 2023.

ISBN: 979-8223938903

Written by JC Ballard.

For Mom & Dad. Thanks for believing in me.

I'M LOST

This isn't what I wanted. Not today. Not ever.

Friday night. I'm supposed to be home, in bed, my sweet patch-coated tabby cat curled up at my feet. At the same time, I enjoy a good book or out with my friends, watching some lousy creature feature at the dollar theater and making fun of it over salty popcorn and sour candy, not laying in a crumpled heap on cold, wet concrete after drinking too much at my best friend's boyfriend's house party.

Everything aches. My head spins. I can hardly catch my breath. The fall must've knocked the wind clear from my lungs.

I sit up to collect myself and get my bearings before a shiver trickles down my spine. I'm not dressed to be outside like this; my sweater, leggings, socks, and sneakers are soaked by drizzling rain. It would be bad any night, but more so this chilly October evening. I check myself over carefully, finding some nasty scrapes on my arms and a worse one on my forehead. Do I have a concussion?

I don't know. I don't want to know. I want to know where I am, but nothing looks familiar, and my head hurts so bad I don't think I could read the street signs even if they did. I feel around for anything; my purse, phone, even my car keys, but I come up empty. I scan my surroundings as best I can, fighting the pounding headache to look for my friend.

Gina. Gina left the party with me. She should be here somewhere, but I don't see her either. Did she leave me when I fell?..did she really leave with me?

I want to go home.

But where is home?

I force myself to my feet, struggling as my head spins harder, and look at the crossroads I find myself at. There's a sidewalk to my right and street lights marking the path. I can almost make out the street sign — maybe I'll recognize it?

To my left...I can't quite tell. The street lights haven't come on that way, but I see something shapeless lying there. Something green. My purse, maybe? And my purse means my phone.

●○●○●○●○●○●

GO RIGHT (page 3) or **GO LEFT (page 5)**

RIGHT

I may be a bumbling and potentially-concussion-stricken mess, but I'm not stupid enough to walk alone in the dark to get what might be my purse or might be a trap set by some creep waiting for girls to trip and fall on wet cement. Besides, as bad as my head hurts, I'm not sure I could make it that far in the dark without stumbling over my feet again anyway. No, my safest bet is walking this way if I want to get home.

But it feels like what looked like it couldn't be more than a few feet of concrete stretches infinitely longer under my unsteady feet. I use the red brick wall lining the sidewalk to keep myself upright, my body growing heavier with each step, one foot in front of the other, until I'm looking up at the green street sign that teased me from the crossroads. H. Hound's Way.

It's official. I hit my head harder than I thought if that's what I'm reading.

I step closer to the sign, leaning my forehead against the slick metal in hopes of easing the relentless pounding. It helps my eyes focus long enough to see clearly, just under my feet, red and lots of it. It pools around my sneakers, the rubber all that stands between the white fabric and permanent stains.

My eyes follow the trail, searching for the source. It could be paint, I tell myself. Red paint for red bricks...but the sinking feeling in my stomach tells me it's something much worse. I follow the trail with my eyes further and farther away until finally focusing on the edge of a ditch. A grassy ditch soaked red, with a gray combat boot sticking straight out. I feel the acid in my stomach rising to my throat. I know I should stay put, and I wish I could.

But I know that boot, and I know there's a body attached to the boot.

Gina's body.

●○●○●○●○●○●

CALL FOR HELP (page 7) or **SAVE MYSELF (page 9)**

LEFT

The street lights look appealing, but I need my purse. More than that, I need my phone, and the only place my phone could be is in my bag. Walking around a strange neighborhood in the dark during a thunderstorm is an awful idea when I can call for help. I'm not going to risk it when I know I can't.

But it's hard to make myself take the first step into the darkness, knowing I won't be able to see what — if anything — might be lurking there for me. Eventually, fear of being out in the middle of all this for a moment longer than necessary drives me forward, but I regret my decision shortly after.

It's too late to turn back once I'm shrouded in darkness though, and walking towards my bag — even as it seems to drift further away — is really my only option. I keep my eyes forward, watching it instead of listening to the world around me. If I let myself lose focus for even a second, I start to feel like someone's following me. I can almost hear their breath near my ear, though I tell myself it's just the wind.

It is just the wind.

When I finally reach my bag, I'm too relieved to hold it in my hands to even care that it's torn and muddy, like something took a liking to it after I stumbled in the street. I try not to think about that as I dig through it, finding my wallet (thank god!) and my phone, looking worse for wear because of the rain but still willing to power on for me.

I check it for a signal, which holds firm, but the battery is nearly dead. I've probably only got one call left. I need to make it count.

●○●○●○●○●○●

CALL MY FRIENDS (page 11) or **CALL MY DAD (page 13)**

CALL FOR HELP

Most people facing a life-or-death situation would weigh every option before making a decision, especially when said decision could end up putting them into the same dire situation. Still, I can't do that, not with Gina.

Gina was destined to be my best friend when her parents found out she was a girl because her mom was my mom's best friend. Gina, who punched nine-year-old Eli Cole in the face during fourth-grade art class after he dumped the paint in my lap because 'he liked me.' Gina, who never shied away from telling me just how bad I looked in salmon pink before senior prom.

I scramble to find the missing phone in my gray sweater pockets, then check my boots even though my pace hurts every bone in my body, but I can't find it. I wish now that I'd gone back to get my bag, or what I thought might be my bag anyway, because maybe my phone was in there. Or maybe not. I could've left the damn thing at the party. I don't remember.

I guess it doesn't matter.

What does matter is Gina is bleeding out and there's nothing I can do about it.

I force myself to move, kneeling beside the ditch and biting back the urge to retch as I take hold of her foot. I pull as hard as I can, desperate to get her body out of the ditch that's rapidly filling with rainwater, but she's so heavy, water-logged from the same rain threatening to keep me down, and I can barely muster the strength to walk this far. I grit my teeth anyway and continue to pull, ignoring the blood that seeps into my jeans as I finally free her from the ditch.

I hold tight to my friend, holding her head against my chest. I don't know what to do, but I can't let Gina die. Not here. Not like this.

●○●○●○●○●○●

CHECK HER BREATHING (page 17) or **STOP THE BLEEDING (page 15)**

SAVE MYSELF

All I've ever imagined, from the day my mom read me fantastic stories about knights and dragons and good and evil until I fell asleep, was that someday I'd get to be just like the heroes she'd tell me about. This is my chance. My best friend is in dire need of help. No one else around to save the day, only me. Gina needs me to act, to save her, and I want to.

God, I want to.

But I can't. I hate myself for it the second I put my foot down in the opposite direction, doubling back the way I came. I don't want to be the hero if it means dying beside her and the only thing I can do is run. Run fast, run far, until this all becomes a distant dream.

What I don't know, as I run from the scene of the crime, is that whatever attacked my friend prefers the hunt over easy prey. I give him what he wants when I take off, and he's more than happy to chase after me in turn. Not that I care. I'm too busy trying to figure out how to survive this mess of my own.

He's experienced, which doesn't help me either. He knows exactly which ways potential victims turn when faced with a crossroads, how to trip them up, and where best to drive his claws to silence their screams. What he doesn't know...is that I'm not like his other victims. Because I know he's after me, and I do something he doesn't expect.

I jump the red-bricked wall, race up the steps of someone's porch, and scream when he drags me back down them. My screams as thick claws pierce my skin alerts the family inside. The oldest son, an ex-marine, comes out with a gun and fires a warning shot into my attacker, saving my life before he calls an officer to take him away.

Their help comes too late to save Gina. My attacker promises I'll regret my choices that got him caught. At least, that's what everyone who reported on the story says. I don't think much about it.

Until the next time, I find myself standing in the dark on H. Hound Way.

●○●○●○●○●○●

Want to see the other endings?
Go back to the start and take another trip through Hellhound's Delight!

CALL MY FRIENDS

I can't be far from the house party, even if I'm not sure where the house is, so my friends won't be far either. I scroll through my contacts, pausing over 'Dad' before I commit to calling a friend. Gina, who dragged me to this stupid party in the first place. She got me into this mess, so I decided she was the right person to rescue me from it.

I hit the green button beside Gina's number, anxiously tapping my foot while I wait for her to answer the damn phone. She's not much help when she does respond, her voice sounding tinny as she promises to send a car in my direction once I turn my location on.

Oddly, she doesn't even care to come to check on me, but I don't waste much thought on it. She's obsessed with her new boyfriend, our party host, and likely doesn't want to run out on him. Even if it is to check on her lifelong best friend, I'm not bitter.

I'm a little bitter.

"Sorry."

"It's fine." It's not. I'm annoyed when the car pulls up and asks for me by name. "I'll see you tomorrow."

My phone dies as I cross the door's threshold, but I dismiss the omen, far more focused on giving the driver my address. I realize too late that my driver isn't... typical—skeletal features, glowing red eyes, and a cackle that could put fear in the dead.

"Where are we going?"

"Home, my dear."

I realize then I won't be seeing Gina tomorrow. A strange sort of calm washes over me while I stare out the window, watching my hometown shrink in the distance as we drift closer and closer to what comes next. I wonder if my parents will look for me.

"They won't need to, dear."

Because Gina — the real Gina, not the ghostly siren calling my soul home after the worst night of my short-lived life — has already found what's left of me.

●○●○●○●○●○●

Want to see the other endings?
Go back to the start and take another trip through Hellhound's Delight!

CALL MY DAD

Look. I get it. I messed up. There's no other way to describe the situation I find myself in, and I don't want to call anyone to rescue me. Especially Dad. He always says, "I want you to call me first if you're in trouble, and I'll come, no questions asked," but I don't think anyone in history ever believed their parents when they said the same thing. Not that I have many options.

So, I suck it up and hit the sugary-sweet photo of us as a kid, then bring the phone to my ear. I'm impatient as the familiar ring buzzes in my ear, tapping my foot and shivering as more winter rain downpours — adding an unnatural chill to my misery.

I sigh with relief for the first time tonight when I hear someone fumbling on the other end to answer the call. His voice is rough. I know I've woken him from a dead sleep, and I'll pay for it when he gets here. "Hello? Who is this?"

"Funny, Dad. It's me," I say, hoping that the sound of his little girl's teeth chattering will earn me some pity points. "Can you come pick me up?"

I don't hear his answer, too focused on the feeling of something brushing lazily against my leg. Knowing I shouldn't, I look down and find the most enormous tail of any animal I've ever seen resting against me. When I look up, I can't help but scream because I'm looking into the solid ice-blue eyes of a rain-soaked black dog much bigger than I am.

●○●○●○●○●○●

HOLD STILL (page 19) or **RUN AWAY (page 21)**

STOP THE BLEEDING

Gina's my best friend. I can't lose her like this, and I'm willing to do whatever it takes to save her. Even sacrifice my favorite purple scarf if it means she'll have a chance. I pull it off my neck and press it to her own; it doesn't take long for the material to grow heavy with her blood. It's all I can do to focus on the task I've assigned myself, even though I'm positive her breathing seems to slow even more if she is breathing at all.

If I knew where my phone was, or Gina's, I'd call for help. I'd beg someone to save us, my friend before she dies on a dark street in the middle of a rainstorm. She deserves so much better than this, but I have nothing better for her—just my sobs as the thunder roars and crackles around us.

So heavy is my despair that I don't realize how close whatever did this to Gina really is, creeping up behind me to inflict the same misfortune in his agitated state. It doesn't matter. The namesake hellhound of H. Hound Way is watching from the shadows and is angry. Too much innocent blood was spilled tonight. It makes quick work of the villain, leaving him a barely recognizable, mauled mess of flesh and bone before it disappears into the night once again.

I lose track of the hours we sit there on the street, sobbing until my face is raw and throat hoarse before paramedics arrive. They have to peel me off my dead friend's body. They have to peel the splattered remains of the monster who did this to her off the concrete. I don't know what to tell them when they ask me what happened. They wouldn't believe me if I did.

A week later, news stations are calling it a tragedy. I call it mercy.

Because it is mercy, he doesn't have to live with the daily reminder of what happened to Gina. I do.

When I return to H. Hound Way someday, I can only hope that the hellhound will lift the Veil and allow me the justice Gina's memory so profoundly deserves.

●○●○●○●○●○●

Want to see the other endings?
Go back to the start and take another trip through Hellhound's Delight!

CHECK HER BREATHING

Come on Gina. It can't end like this. Not this way.

My face grows warm, hot tears mixing with cold rainwater and dripping down my friend's pale face. I don't know what to do. I don't know how to help her or even know if she's alive. I don't know anything except...

Except...except, my neck feels warm. Strangely warm. I blink twice, clearing as many tears from my eyes as I can, and focus on Gina. What I hear, what I see, what I feel — and I can feel her breath on my neck. Shallow breaths. She's alive.

I lay Gina's limp body on the concrete as gently as I could, then pressed my head against her chest. I do everything I can to ignore the thick smell of blood that surrounds Gina, ignoring the desire to dry-heave while I listen for a heartbeat. The hand that isn't lying on her shoulder finds her wrist, timing her pulse as best I can despite an evident inability to focus, not that it helps me much. I'm not a nursing student and don't know what to do in situations like this.

At least I know she's alive, though she won't be for much longer if I let her weakened heart continue pumping blood straight out of her body. I struggle to shrug my way out of my sweater before pressing the wool against her chest. I don't know if it's enough to stop what's been done, but I take this brief reprise from imminent danger to look around. If Gina's still alive, then whatever attacked her only just got to her. And if that's true, whatever attacked Gina might still be nearby. Like this, we're easy targets. Very easy targets.

But we're not alone, not really. There's a house nearby, the house with the red brick wall. Surely they'll have a phone. If I tie my sweater tight enough around Gina's chest, I can get help...but can I really leave my best friend here in the middle of the street? What if it comes back to finish the job?

●○●○●○●○●○●

TRY TO GET HELP (page 25) or **STAY WITH GINA (page 23)**

HOLD STILL

I wonder why people always say, "It's more afraid of you than you are of it," when they're talking about a predator that wouldn't hesitate to hurt you before you hurt it. When did we decide that, and who knows if it's true? I promise you, this giant hound isn't afraid of me. If it's thinking anything about me, I'm either its dinner or its next chew toy — neither option appeals to me.

Don't panic. Don't panic.

Well, maybe not dinner since it's acting like it doesn't even realize I'm here so long as I hold still and make no sudden movements. Like dropping my purse when it lifts a paw and swats at it, but even then, it's more interested in sticking its nose there to inspect the contents.

Should I tell him there's no food?

I make a strange noise — a cross between a laugh and a sob — and the hound's attention returns to me briefly after pulling its head from my purse pockets. It tilts its head, regarding me with glowing blue eyes, before nipping my sweater. I'd almost think it was being careful, trying to avoid skin with its teeth, before it tugs down gently. Barely enough for me to feel it, but firm enough to get my attention.

Why?

Because it wants me to go somewhere. With it. Alone.

●○●○●○●○●○●

FOLLOW HIM (page 27) or **REFUSE (page 29)**

RUN AWAY

I won't pretend to know anything about dogs — wolves? No, this looks more dog-like than wolf-like, but it is wolf-sized...well, I guess it doesn't really matter what it is when it's large enough to eat me. Not in one bite (that's ridiculous!), but it could probably do it in three. So, I do the only thing that makes sense. I turn back towards the street lights and scream while running for my life.

I'm so distressed, understandably given the circumstances, that I don't hear Dad on the other end. He's frightened for me, tugging on his boots, grabbing his gun, and begging me to tell him what's wrong until my phone dies. Not that it matters anymore. The hound gives chase, running half-speed to tease me because it knows I won't really outrun it.

Not for lack of trying. I round the first corner, crossing over the spot I woke up in not long ago. Behind me, I hear barking, like it's laughing at me, before I round a second corner, then a third, until I finally slip on slick concrete and tumble off the sidewalk, into someone's yard.

I grunt, rolling myself over in the muddy grass to see the starry sky when the hound catches me...but it never comes. I shift just enough to look around, finding no great beast. Just a house, with loud music and people pouring from every entrance. The house party. Great.

Not that it matters. No one notices me while I lay there in the rain, waiting for someone I know to come to save me. And who is the hero of the evening?

Dad. He's angry about being woken up, and having to hear me scream when there wasn't anything he could do about it, and seeing me all banged up and muddy when I was meant to be safe inside with my friends, but he's glad I'm okay. He says we'll talk about the rest in the morning.

I don't argue, and I don't say anything about the hound. I know he won't understand, but I know what I say. I'll be back tomorrow, sober, to prove it.

●○●○●○●○●○●

Want to see the other endings?
Go back to the start and take another trip through Hellhound's Delight!

STAY WITH GINA

I don't have the strength to beg for Gina to fight. She's basically dead already, no matter how hard I press the sweater to her wounds to keep some of her blood in her body. I know it. I think Gina knows it too. Maybe that's why she musters the last of her strength to brush her bloody hand against my arm.

Is it a last request? Her begging me to run and save myself as she breathes her last breath? It doesn't matter. I couldn't run if I wanted to. I have to be here, so she doesn't die alone. And die she does. The death rattle of her ruined lungs haunts me, unfocused eyes staring straight into my soul.

I didn't save her. Maybe I never could.

But it doesn't matter. Gina deserves peace, even in death, and I muster all my courage to move my hand toward her bloody face. I bite back any urge to gag or retch, unwilling to add to my friend's suffering, as I touch her cold face. Trembling fingers settle on her eyelids as I force them closed, allowing her a dreamless sleep in death's embrace.

This isn't right. We shouldn't be here.

But I can let myself grieve without her cold, dead eyes staring at me, for as long as I can. Not that I get much more than a single, solitary heartbeat to myself before a lone howl calls from the forest. Whatever took my friend isn't finished yet. He's come back for me.

Staying sealed my death certificate.
I never make it home.

●○●○●○●○●○●

Want to see the other endings?
Go back to the start and take another trip through Hellhound's Delight!

TRY TO GET HELP

I love Gina. I'd give up anything to save her. She knows that, and she'd understand the last thing I want to do is leave her here, but she needs help I can't give her. She needs someone who can save her life, with blood, stitches, and antibiotics after lying in that ditch for who knows how long. Our only chance is a phone call. I need to find a phone.

I force every inch of my body to fight the instinct to stay by her side, the only instinct I'd ever imagine I'd have, and it's just enough to get my legs underneath me again. I ignore the squelching sound of blood squishing around my feet and turn back towards the red brick wall. If I can get to the wall, I can get up their driveway and to the porch. But will they help me?

I can't think about that now. All that matters is getting to their front door. I can worry about the rest later.

That's what I think, anyway, but I don't get far before I feel someone take hold of my leg. I scream, looking down to stomp on whatever has hold of me, but all it does is send me to the ground, hard, into the puddle of blood. I scramble, trying to crawl away, but the hand holds tighter to my leg, a grip so unforgiving I worry it'll break bone if I continue to resist. Another hand grabs my other leg, holding me there, and whatever it is growls my name.

I swallow hard, forcing myself to face whatever it is that's decided I'm its next meal, and choke out a sob when I see for myself. Gina, pale as a ghost, drowning in her own blood, clinging to me with an otherworldly gaze in her bloodshot green eyes.

Green eyes?

Not brown. Green. Wolfish green eyes.

This isn't Gina. Is it?

●○●○●○●○●○●

SCREAM (**page 35**) or **HUG HER** (**page 37**)

FOLLOW HIM

Look. I get it. I've made a lot of bad decisions that led me to this moment. No one ever wakes up one day and thinks, "I'm going to put myself in the path of the largest black dog I've ever seen." Not that I really believe this is my fault. Who would ever imagine an invitation to a simple house party would set me here, in front of said hound, trying to nudge me along instead of eat me?

I weigh my options, but I don't think I have a choice here, and it's probably best not to argue. *What's the worst that could happen?*

Oh...right. I could still be eaten. Mom would kill me if she had to plan a funeral this week (well, more so than she's already going to kill me after all the trouble I've gotten into).

But the hound is impatient, nudging me more insistently now that it assumes I've made my decision. I start to move, even though my legs ache terribly from all the exercise I've done tonight. I follow the giant beast over the fence between the street and the clearing, then deep into the forested tree line, far from the beaten path.

I chuckle at the irony, much to the hound's dismay. I'm quickly becoming Little Red Riding Hood, but the wolf is less predator than you'd expect. For now. Definitely not forever; I'm under no illusions of safety whenever the hound gets me wherever it wants to go.

After what feels like hours of walking, we come to a temporary stop beside a winding river I've never seen or heard of before. It stops at the riverbank, inspecting the silver-gray water before dipping down for a long drink. Then, it sits back on its heels to watch me. I step closer to the river and its ears perk, eager to see what I'll do next. But what will I do next?

●○●○●○●○●○●

SIT DOWN (page 31) or **DRINK (page 33)**

REFUSE

I want to scream, but I don't want to risk angering the hound any more than I've already done by taking two giant steps away from it. The hound huffs at me, indignant at my refusal, and nudges my arm a second time. I don't look into its eyes, taking my bag from its teeth and shouldering it instead.

It makes another noise I can only associate with annoyance before padding away like it's going to find another lost soul in the dark. I don't care. I'd much rather it leave me alone in the dark than continue lurking like it's hungry (or worse, hasn't decided whether it is).

Alone again, I wonder if I should've followed it. I make a bad decision at that moment, calling out to it again, hoping briefly it will return and keep me company until I find my way home.

What? I'm a dog person.

The hound doesn't return, so I do the next best thing. I wander around the empty streets for hours until my feet are sore and ache with exhaustion.

Muddy and tired, I take a seat against a fence nearby and close my eyes. It isn't until I wake in the morning that I realize I've found my way home, that it was my fence I slept against last night.

It doesn't make sense. I don't know how I made it home, but I don't complain. I go inside to my own warm bed. I forget about the party and the wolf so I can sleep.

●○●○●○●○●○●

Want to see the other endings?
Go back to the start and take another trip through Hellhound's Delight!

SIT DOWN

I'm thirsty. I know I want a drink, no matter what's been taking drinks from the river, but I can't bring myself to take one. Something about the silver pool of rushing water scares me, deep in my soul. My hound led me here for a reason, but I can't do what it wants. I won't.

Instead, I sit beside the river and watch it flow. Someone will come looking for me when the sun rises and my parents realize I didn't come home. If I stay here long enough, they'll find me.

But the hound doesn't accept my answer. It growls when I refuse its offering, pacing the area around me over and over again. It offers me another drink. Again I refuse and, in the grips of its rage, the hound's massive body forces mine into the silver river.

It burns like acid when I hit the water, flesh melting away and fur taking its place. I fight the rapids back towards the shore, desperate to claw my way from its grip. Literally, because I can feel dark claws where fingernails used to be digging into the mud to keep me from being tugged back into the river.

I turn towards the hound, my own massive form nearly dominating its own. I catch a glimpse of myself in the water and howl with despair. I match my companion now, the same glowing eyes and coarse black fur. The river changed me into the same omen that's haunted me tonight, a follower of Death himself.

I should've stayed home.

●○●○●○●○●○●

Want to see the other endings?
Go back to the start and take another trip through Hellhound's Delight!

DRINK

My throat is dry, and the bits of rainwater I've managed to moisten my tongue with on our walk to the river are only just enough to keep me from coughing. I know I need a drink soon, and I trust an animal's instinct on what's safe and what's not...well, I trust that it's still standing after taking a drink.

Bottom's up.

I kneel beside the river and dip my hands into its silvery depths, bringing cool water up to my lips. I drink, desperate for the relief it brings, and sigh softly as the hound howls beside me. I look up and see the moon, smiling briefly when I know the rain has finally stopped pouring, leaving me and my hound alone in the cool winter air.

Relief lasts for a moment, maybe more, before the river water droplets burn at my skin. My insides catch fire and I collapse in the mud, writhing in pain. My hound howls again as I gasp for air, choking out weak pleas with some inhumane force for mercy, for relief, for death if it means the pain will end.

The sky is still a sickening pitch-blue when my agony ends slowly, and I feel like I can stand once more. My hound smiles as it creeps to my side, otherworldly eyes regarding me as I look to the river.

I catch a glimpse of something, a reflection that looks somewhat like my own, but it can't be. This figure is near translucent, a ghost, with muddy robes instead of a muddy sweater. I blink. It disappears, leaving me and my hound. "What did you do to me?"

The hound doesn't answer. It smiles sharply instead and I worry. *What does it mean?*

●○●○●○●○●○●

I'M DEAD (page 47) or **I'M DREAMING (page 49)**

SCREAM

It's not Gina. I knew it wasn't the moment I saw those bloodshot green eyes, but I wanted to believe it. For even a second, I wanted to believe she was there and she was alive and this wasn't all some terrible trick. But it's not her.

I don't know what's going to happen when I scream, but I do it anyway. I open my mouth to do it, which counts for something. Not much, given that I don't manage to make a noise with Gina's (not Gina's?) hand clamped tight over my mouth. She's smothering me, preventing me from screaming for help. It only frightens me more.

Gina would never do something like this to me, frighten me after I managed to pull her out of a ditch after she's been attacked. Hell, after I was attacked? Who's to say that whatever got to not-Gina didn't attack me first? Maybe that's why I was lying on the pavement with a concussion and no memory of how I got there or where my purse and phone went.

"I need you to calm down," Gina says with a growl. Her green eyes won't leave mine, but it's of little comfort. This abomination wearing my friend's face doesn't seem to know what color her eyes are meant to be and I'm half-tempted to sink my teeth into her hand if it means she'll let me go. "Something bit me."

Her hand lightens the pressure against my face for only a second before it increases even more. She sounds like Gina, but she doesn't feel like Gina anymore. Whatever it is that bit her, if something bit her and this is actually her, changed her in ways I don't understand. Maybe I can't understand anymore.

"I need help. Please," Gina says, a softer approach this time. "I'll move my hand, but you have to be quiet. Understand?"

I nod. Whether I mean it is another story.

●○●○●○●○●○●

STAY QUIET (**page 39**) or **SCREAM ANYWAY** (**page 41**)

HUG HER

"I thought I'd lost you," I say, wrapping my arms around her tight, in hopes she'll understand how scared I am. Maybe I shouldn't. Maybe I should take a step back and evaluate the situation, but that's not how brains work when they're distressed. "Are you hurt?"

I expect an answer from my bleeding friend, but what comes instead is a vice grip on my hips. Gina didn't hesitate to throw me off, wild eyes focused on me as I attacked her. Like I've caged her in a place and time she no longer belongs to. Her newly-changed green eyes glow with otherworldly hate and something more, something almost human. An emotion I recognize. A sentiment I share — fear. She's afraid.

So am I.

Gina claws at her throat now that she's free from my arms, trying to tell me something I don't understand. She's panicking now, digging her nails deep into the skin of her neck, trying to free herself from whatever is lurking in her mind. I can't sit there doing nothing while my friend suffers, so I move closer. It pulls her from the heightened haze, establishing me as her enemy a second time. She growls, a low guttural thing I never want to hear again.

It chills me deeper than the cold rain ever could and I need to do something to help her before she makes a terrible decision

— or an unforgivable mistake. I look for her phone, sure the bright pink phone case will be obvious enough that I can find it, even if it's stuck in the mud. Gina doesn't like me moving around and grabs at me. "I'm trying to help you."

●○●○●○●○●○●

LOOK FOR HER PHONE (**page 45**) or **HELP HER STAND** (**page 43**)

STAY QUIET

Everything I've done so far, I've done to help myself and help Gina. I don't even have to ask what she'd do if situations were reversed; she'd bend over backward to save me by whatever means necessary. This may not be Gina. I know that, and it scares me — but I have to keep doing whatever keeps me alive, so I can find Gina and save her like she'd save me.

I've made my choice. No turning back now.

Gina waits for any indication I'll do something different, something that will make her mad before she pulls her hand away and waits for the scream she's sure I'll make. None comes, and she smiles. A strange smile with canines sharper than any I've seen from her smile before. I try to hide those emotions best I can. I know how dangerous predators can be; predators trapped or cornered can be even worse. I never imagined I'd think of Gina this way, but what else can I do?

This isn't Gina, remember?

No. I don't remember, but I need to do something more than sit here and stare at her. I stand, feeling her eyes follow every move I make, ready to take hold of my legs if it stops me from running. Not that I would ever run from whatever she is, not when I don't know if she could catch me or not. "What are you doing?"

"Standing up," I whisper, scared the slightest noise might set her off. "I can't sit in your blood anymore, Gina." She nods. She can understand that, even if she doesn't understand much else. "What happened to you?"

"I don't know. I can hear everything, and smell everything around me. It's too much to bear," Gina cries. "I can hardly breathe. It hurts so bad. And I can feel-."

"Feel?"

"A presence, a whisper in my head. Something I can't explain." The presence, she goes on, is a constant growl in the back of her mind. It won't leave her alone, endlessly searching for its next meal. "Help me."

●○●○●○●○●○●

PROMISE TO HELP HER (**page 61**) or **APOLOGIZE & LEAVE** (**page 59**)

SCREAM ANYWAY

It's a betrayal. I know it is long before I scream, but I can't stop myself. I'm afraid of whatever it is in front of me, whether it's Gina or something worse, and I can't sit there in silence. Much as I want to do anything else, like not betray my best friend (if this is still my best friend) on what's probably the worst day of her life, the shrill scream escapes when her hand moves is the only thing I can do.

"Help! Please, someone, help me! My friend is dead," I scream. I scream as loud as I can, hoping someone somewhere is listening and will come to my rescue. But no one does. It's only Gina and me forever, in a moment that only ends when she snarls. "Gina, no, please-."

She rips the words from my throat in an instant, my screaming only accomplishing one goal — irritating her sensitive hearing because she doesn't know how to react. She needs me to stop, to be quiet, and there's only one way that makes sense to her now. Impossibly sharp teeth sink into my neck, sending intense pain through my entire body.

... ...

I understand now. What happened to Gina wasn't death; it was life. Life as something new, something dangerous — something more substantial than mere mortals could ever be. I feel it coursing through my veins, an ethereal understanding of this power when she finally releases my neck.

She apologizes, but there's no need. Not now, because I understand. We are part of the darkness now, together, forever.

We disappear after that, leaving town together so we don't run the risk of forcing this new power on anyone else. Our families report us to the police, leaving us known as runaways. No one else is turned in our sleepy little town.

At least, not yet.

●○●○●○●○●○●

Want to see the other endings?
Go back to the start and take another trip through Hellhound's Delight!

HELP HER STAND

I'll admit, when I woke up this morning, I didn't think that this was how my day would play out. Cold, wet, covered in blood while I try to help my best friend after she's been brutally attacked — who most adamantly doesn't want my help in any form or fashion. Of course, I don't know just how badly she doesn't like my help until I force myself to stand, then try to help her do the same.

I should've left her alone.

That's all I can think about as she forces me backward, sending me deep into the ditch beside us. I groan from the impact, finding myself stuck in the mud and pooling rainwater. Gina doesn't seem to care as she descends on the ditch more gracefully than she allows, approaching me with a deep hunger in her eyes.

Before I can react, Gina is on top of me, sinking her sharp teeth into my neck. No, not teeth. Those aren't teeth anymore. Those are fangs. Impossibly sharp fangs that she's using to drain me of blood. And, when she's done, she discards me in the ditch once more. She doesn't care about the mud keeping me stuck in place as more rainwater fills the pool. "I'm sorry," she says in something more or less like a hiss. I don't know that she means it. "I wanted you to stay away."

The sudden blood infusion seems to calm her, but it makes me dizzy and lightheaded. I try to sit up and ask questions anyway, not that I can make much of a sound. Gina doesn't care; she knows it's too late to go back now. She apologizes again and leaves me in the ditch. To die? No. I'm not that lucky. She's left me here to change. Change into whatever she's been transformed into.

I watch her disappear from view, heading deep into the trees, and allow the mud to claim me as its victim until morning, when a jogger happens by and takes pity on my sorry self.

I never see Gina again. I don't know where she is. I don't even know if she's alive. I don't care either way; she can stay in hiding for the rest of our very long lives if she knows what's good for her.

●○●○●○●○●○●

Want to see the other endings?
Go back to the start and take another trip through Hellhound's Delight!

LOOK FOR HER PHONE

Her phone might be in her pocket. How I would get it out with her watching my every move is a problem of its own, but...well, given that my phone has been missing since I opened my eyes, it's our best chance at getting us both out of this situation alive. "What's that?" I ask, pointing off into the distance — a distraction that works better than I thought.

Gina's head turns, leaving me able to surge forward and push her flat against the pavement. I don't have much time, using my legs to pin her arms down so there's no chance of her hurting me in a fit of startled rage. My shaking hands find her black jean jacket, turning out each pocket and coming up empty, but I don't give up there. She's got plenty of other pockets to tear open.

I move from her jacket to the pockets of her jeans. Her blood has soaked into them, just as it has mine, leaving my hands slicker than before. I'd be disgusted if I weren't so angry that her phone wasn't in any of those pockets either. I groan under my breath before I move, pulling my weight off Gina and startling her as she snaps at me.

I can't focus on being offended for long. When she pushes me off her, sending me into the pavement as punishment for doing it to her, she also puts me right beside the very thing I'd been looking for. It's a good thing Gina can't keep passwords a secret to save her life. She loves numeric passwords that spell something. In this case...

5. 6. 8. 3.

L. O. V. E.

I don't love her for putting me in this situation right now, but at least I can finally call for help. Maybe we'll get to go home soon.

●○●○●○●○●○●

CALL 911 (**page 57**) or **CALL HER PARENTS** (**page 55**)

I'M DEAD

Dead. Dying. Deader. There's no other explanation for what's happened to me, no other way to explain the horrible fate I find myself facing. Not that my hound cares much for my suffering or pain. It only manages to be amused, and it is very much amused. My death is all it wanted.

What are my parents going to do? Will anyone find my body? Do I even know where my body is? I look around, searching for answers in the black hound's eyes, and scream as it smiles with those crooked sharp teeth, ready to silence my soul forever.

BRNNNNNGG.

I yawn in the midst of my panic.

BRNNNNNGG.

I sit up slowly and look around. I'm not in a clearing, by a river, with a hound. I'm in my bedroom; I'd known that faded turquoise walls and outdated boy band posters anywhere. Everything is exactly how I left it when I went to bed last night like nothing happened.

I'm safe.

I'm home.

It was all a dream.

...I think.

I hope...

●○●○●○●○●○●

Want to see the other endings?
Go back to the start and take another trip through Hellhound's Delight!

I'M DREAMING

I'm dreaming.

That's the only way to explain all these things happening to me. Right? Yes, right. The hound, the party, the water, Gina — it's all just symbolism in my subconscious pointing to issues with my life outside my dreams. I laugh again, comforted by the reality I paint for myself.

I pinch my arm to prove it, but nothing happens. I look in the river again; I pray being aware it's a dream will set something straight, but no luck there either. My skin, still pale, and my clothes, still muddy. No black and purple floral pajamas in sight.

I look to my hound for answers. None come. Instead, it leaves me sitting beside the river, alone once more. I don't know where to go or what to do next without my hound dragging me along. I just want to go home and lie down in my bed, after I've had a long shower. Is that so much to ask?

"Of course, little one. You're not quite there yet."

I startle at the sound and look around the riverbank for the source of the ethereal voice haunting my thoughts. I don't see anyone or anything, but a light. A small light, further into the forest. It dances before me, beckoning me across the river. "Closer, closer," it teases me. "Ever closer now."

I know better now about following things I don't understand, but I don't feel like I have a choice. I need to keep going and see what this dream (*please be a dream!*) has left in store for me. I follow the light along the river, through one forest past a rocky field, and into another until we reach a cliffside. I hear the roar of a great waterfall but see none nearby. I know there aren't waterfalls this close to town.

The light doesn't care, drifting down towards the water, before disappearing beneath the dark waves of silver water.

●○●○●○●○●○●

JUMP (page 53) or **GO BACK (page 51)**

GO BACK

I'm not stupid enough to jump but not smart enough to remember the way out of the forest. The best I can do is walk back the way I can until I find the street or the hound. I don't love the idea of the hound being my best option, but it was friendly enough to lead me here and is far less frightening than cold ocean water at the bottom of a cliff. Maybe it'll take me home.

Well, probably not, but I don't have better options. I trek through the trees, back through the clearing, following the river back to where I last saw my hound. It's gone, long gone, so I keep going. I look for some marker, something to point me back to the street. After hours of stumbling, I finally emerged from the trees and onto the pavement. My house sits on the other side of the road.

I rush across the street, up the steps, and look inside the window. I see my parents crying on the couch, an officer sitting patiently in the armchair, talking gently to them

This isn't right.

I push the door open and go inside to greet them. No one jumps up when they hear the door, but it doesn't matter as I reach the living room and throw myself onto the couch to hug them...sinking straight through it. They didn't hear me, didn't see me. They didn't even feel me fall through them. I push myself up, escaping the view of inside my childhood couch and all the disgusting snacks and dirty coins lost to it over the year.

My stomach twists as I see what they saw, a photograph between the officer's fingers. A young woman's body was found on the side of the road. Dead, no cause of death. My body. My death.

"Mom, mom. It's okay. I'm right here," I insist, trying to grip her hand and watching mine slip through it instead. "Momma, please. Please."

But she still doesn't see me. They never see me, even as I lurk in the window and watch the moving van pull away from the house three years after my death. It leaves me tethered to the empty shell of our former home as they start a new life, far away from where I died.

●○●○●○●○●○●

Want to see the other endings?
Go back to the start and take another trip through Hellhound's Delight!

JUMP

The strangest dream I've ever had...wasn't actually all that different from this. Of course, I was wearing blue spandex with a cape, standing on the edge of a skyscraper, and I could fly, but still. Not that different. I didn't go 'splat' on the sidewalk in that dream. I know I won't drown in this one.

Besides, as I said...it's just a dream. Nothing can hurt me when I'm dreaming; it might just be enough to scare me awake when I hit the water. I step closer to the edge of the cliff, peering down into a dark ocean of silver. Even in dreams, I know this isn't a good idea.

Am I really crazy enough to go through with this?

Am I really about to jump?

Is this really my only way home?

Yes. I know in my heart that it's my only way home. These forces mean to tell me something, something my subconscious thinks I need to know. I take a deep breath, get a running start, and feel my feet leave the ground when I finally force myself to take that leap.

I hover for a second, no longer on land but not quite in the sea, before plummeting down toward the water. Its silver embrace grows closer and closer with each heart-pounding second, as do the rocks lining the shore. I didn't see them before I jumped.

This will hurt.

●○●○●○●○●○●

PUSH OFF THE CLIFFSIDE (page 69) or **CLOSE MY EYES (page 67)**

CALL HER PARENTS

If I were the one sitting with my neck healing in minutes after being torn apart, surrounded by pools of my own blood, unable to speak, the only person in the world I'd want is my dad. Of course, Gina's dad lives in Tampa with a yoga instructor he ditched Gina's mom for almost two years ago...so I obviously call her mom instead.

I sit beside Gina, waiting for her mom to answer the phone so I can explain what's going on (or try, at least). By the time I hear the call connect, all she, I, and Gina can hear is a blood-curdling howl. I shift, coming to face an honest-to-God monster worse than anything I've ever seen in the movies—pitch black fur, blood-red eyes, and paws larger than my face.

Gina cowers, and I understand. This is what attacked her, and it's come back for seconds. *Me.*

A heartbeat passes before the beast leaps toward me, ready for another taste of human flesh. But this time, Gina's ready. Awake, alert, and healing faster than anyone conceivably could, she's prepared to fight back the instant she realizes another life is in danger.

Lightning strikes in the distance, illuminating the wrestling match between woman and wolf, my friend using her newfound strength to hold her own. Claws meet flesh, and fists meet snout, one pummeling blow after another as they push each other across the pavement, adding more blood to the concrete. I'm rooted where I stand, unable to move from fear, until I get caught in the crossfire.

But Gina's ready for that too. In her fury, she manages to stomp the great beast's head with her black combat boots and shove its limp body into the ditch, where it can nurse its wounded pride. Then, she turns her bloodlust gaze to me. For a moment, I worry I'll be next.

Until she shakes herself from it, green eyes turning brown once more. She helps me to my feet and returns her phone to my hand. Her mom is still there, and she's already called the police. They're on their way to wherever it is we are, but Gina insists we should move. She doesn't want us there if whatever she fought crawls out of the ditch.

Fine with me.

I follow her lead down the remaining stretch of street, to a nearby park where we wait for the officers. When they arrive, Gina's injuries are healed and any sign of the struggle on H. Hound Way disappears with them, washed away from bodies, clothes, and concrete by the rain. The officers take us to the hospital where our parents are waiting, even though they don't believe our story about the party, the wolf, or the blood.

My dad promises we're safe here...but with the howling I hear outside my hospital room window, I'm not so sure he's right.

●○●○●○●○●○●

Want to see the other endings?
Go back to the start and take another trip through
Hellhound's Delight!

CALL 911

Everything I know about emergencies — and this is an emergency — means I need to call 911 first. The sooner I get someone here to help Gina, the sooner someone is here to help me, and I'm sure they'll prioritize a mugging (is this a mugging?) over anything else going on tonight.

I can't make any promises to Gina though, watching her from a short distance while I sit and wait for an operator to answer. She doesn't ask me for any, still pawing at her throat occasionally. I wonder if she's been shocked into momentary muteness, or if something far worse is happening that I haven't realized yet.

She's been resistant to touch since I pulled her from the ditch, but I hate sitting here while she's distressed. So, against my better judgment, I reach over and set my hand on hers while I listen to the busy signal. I hang up and try again. Then again. And again. And a fourth time for the fun of it.

It's only when I call a fifth, sixth, and seventh time that an operator finally answers the phone (and I force myself to bite back any scathing comments about their wasting time). Instead, I tell them that my friend was attacked, I don't know where we are, and there's so much blood.

The operator asks questions. I answer them as best I can. He asks more questions after that, keeping me on the phone long enough that he finally figures out where we are and sends paramedics our way. I beg him to stay on the phone while we wait; he does, even though there are other calls he could be answering. He knows we're afraid, and he knows waiting where Gina was attacked makes it worse.

Thirty minutes feels like hours before they arrive in the stark white ambulance, illuminating the dark night with their red and blue siren lights. It takes more time for them to put Gina in a neck brace, situate her on a gurney, and place her in the ambulance. The female paramedic asks if I want to ride along to the hospital or wait for an officer to arrive. They're only two minutes away.

●○●○●○●○●○●

AGREE & CLIMB IN (**page 63**) or **REFUSE THE RIDE** (**page 65**)

APOLOGIZE & LEAVE

No one will ever understand what it was like that night, looking at something wearing my best friend's face and begging me for help with her voice, as though I'd fall for the same sort of trick that probably got Gina killed in the first place. I couldn't be part of whatever madness or mania my head injury induces, no matter how much I love Gina.

So I did an awful thing, leaving my "best friend" in a puddle of her own blood and no explanation for what happened to her, to find my own way home. It was the only thing I could do to keep myself alive; otherwise, we'd both be dead in a ditch. Hours passed before I found my way home, and I barely had the strength to peel off my rain-and-blood-soaked clothes before crawling into bed.

… … …

I'm woken the following day by the sound of someone banging at my front door, an officer — holding a picture of Gina from her first day of sophomore year — because she didn't come home last night and her parents know I had to be the last one to see her. It's true, in ways no one will ever know and certainly won't understand.

I try to tell everyone who will listen that something Gina-like was alive when I saw her last and take them to the strange street, by the ditch I pulled her from. They find so much blood on the concrete, in the dirt, splattered across the grass, and soaked in my clothes.

Even though I tell the truth, a truth too strange to make up, no one believes me. I'm the prime suspect in a crime I didn't, couldn't, and wouldn't commit against my best friend. There's going to be a trial. If I tell everyone where the body is, my lawyer thinks they'll go easy on me in sentencing.

I would if I could.

●○●○●○●○●○●

Want to see the other endings?
Go back to the start and take another trip through Hellhound's Delight!

PROMISE TO HELP HER

Gina takes hold of my hand, warmth returning to her skin with each passing moment, her body fighting the cold rain with everything it has as she stands up to face me. She seems taller now than she ever did before, and firmer than I'd expect from someone who lost so much blood. I can't help feeling so much for her in that moment; stranger, monster, or something worse, I can't just forget about someone wearing my friend's face.

I reach forward and peel back the sweater I've tied around her chest, getting a good look at the deep wounds on her neck and chest. What was left of them, anyway. The injuries were already starting to close up, which didn't bother me much. I don't have to worry about trying to explain this to a hospital, though I still think she should go. *Me too. I hit my head pretty hard.*

Not that Gina listens. She cares more about finding her way home now that she's on her feet, using her newly heightened senses to 'guide' them home (something I'm hoping was her way of saying 'I don't have a concussion'). I really didn't like what was going on with her, but I wasn't in much position to put up a fight and Gina finding her way home meant I had a safe place to sleep off whatever happened to me too.

... ...

When I woke the next morning, Gina is nowhere to be found. Her parents don't seem to remember us coming home late the night before and I leave before they're able to fuss over the barely-scabbed-over cut on my forehead to figure out precisely what happened to us on the way home.

But standing on Gina's street, I find myself staring at what looks like my best friend talking to a dog. A big dog with ink-black fur shimmering in the morning sunlight, and eerie blue eyes, seems to understand exactly what she's saying. He doesn't look right, near frightening, and I watch in horror as Gina lets it lead her away. *Where's she going?*

… … …

A week later, I had an answer. Whatever's wearing Gina's face comes home a new person with newfound confidence, new friends just as frightening as she is, and a new wolf-dog pet, who hardly cares to remember my name. I'd muster the energy to be hurt, if I weren't more worried about what happened to the real Gina, what could've happened to me, and why no one else seems to notice or care.

I intend to find out.

●○●○●○●○●○●

Want to see the other endings?
Go back to the start and take another trip through Hellhound's Delight!

AGREE & CLIMB IN

Look. I love horror movies. A lot. So much so that I know all the tips and tricks for surviving at the end, and I promise — sticking around after the ambulance leaves late at night while an attempted murderer might be hiding nearby, waiting for a second chance to attack either one of us, is a bad idea. I think all the genre's bravest and best 'final girls' would be proud.

I accept the paramedic's offer, taking hold of their hand to make it up the steps. I hesitate for a second before they close the doors, thinking about my purse and my phone, lost in the darkness somewhere anyone could pick them up. I explain when the paramedics ask what's wrong and they reassure me, the driver even calls it in, so the officers know to look for it when they arrive.

… … …

A Good Samaritan turns my purse over to an officer in the morning while they investigate the scene. My phone wasn't with it, but I don't care. Better to live without it than die with it. Gina agrees; she's lucky the hospital was able to help her with the shock, which hadn't disappeared with the rest of her wounds.

No one can explain what happened that night. Not Gina, who can't remember anything before she was placed on the gurney. Certainly not me. Had the officers not found all the blood, I don't know if they would've believed something had happened at all.

… … …

Years go by peacefully after Gina's attack. Our sleepy town forgets about whatever attacked Gina, and I'm the only one who wonders if it's still out there. It isn't until another attack occurs on the tenth anniversary that anyone panics...because, this time, the monster — my best friend with her cursed green eyes and wolfish smile — is caught in the act.

●○●○●○●○●○●

Want to see the other endings?
Go back to the start and take another trip through Hellhound's Delight!

REFUSE THE RIDE

I don't want them to leave me here, but I know my purse — meaning my wallet, meaning my ID with my address — is out there somewhere with someone willing to attack innocent women on the street for no reason. I'd rather not wait around and hope for the best. What if they find it and use it to find me, or go after Gina again?

"No. I'll wait."

"Are you sure?"

"Yes."

It isn't until I find my purse lying against a chainlink fence, far from where I woke up, that I realize...*I should've said no.*

... ...

My funeral is a lovely affair, attended by my family and best friend, who mourn a life cut short. The officers who arrived two minutes too late and found my body in a pool of blood were there too. I try to comfort them, explaining that my fate is my fault for refusing the ride.

But I can't. Newly trapped souls can't manifest physically. That's what the other souls the hellhound has trapped in the Veil tell me. They say I'll get used to it eventually. I don't know if they're right, but at least I'm not alone. There are five of us now—five murdered people, five graves, over five decades. No one knows that the beast who took our lives is still out there, lurking in the forest, waiting for its next victim.

Who will join us next?

●○●○●○●○●○●

Want to see the other endings?
Go back to the start and take another trip through Hellhound's Delight!

CLOSE MY EYES

I don't have time to do anything. I can't think. I can't breathe. But I know now this isn't a dream. I would've woken up now if it was, but I haven't. This is real, all of it, and I'm going to die.

If this is how I'm going to die, I don't want to see it.

I force my eyes to close and hold my breath, waiting for my body to crumble against the rocks or water. I wait and wait, but the cruel, crushing impact of bone against rock never comes. Instead, I feel cold as I hit the water. Cold and heavy, then suddenly...hot. Boiling hot, like I'm being burned alive by water.

Shit.

I force my arms forward, then back, over and over again as I swim towards the surface. I need to get out, though I worry the burning might just kill me before anything else can. It takes everything I have to breach the surface and brush the poisoned water from my eyes. And when I do, all I see is light.

Deep blue billowing light, teasing me once more as it dots a perfect path to the shore's edge. The pain falters in its presence, bright, warm, and alluring, and I feel safe despite the crashing waves threatening to throw me into the rocks. I reach for it, groaning in grief as it disappears, leaving me to follow the next one, and the one after that, each wisp of light vanishing before I can feel it on my fingertips.

I won't stop trying to catch them, swimming along the path they set, because I know I can't tread water forever. Each wave threatens to send me under and hold me there until I drown. I only have one path ahead of me — swim to safety — and it's not one with easy options.

●○●○●○●○●○●

FOLLOW THE LIGHTS (page 73) or **SWIM TO SHORE (page 71)**

PUSH OFF THE CLIFFSIDE

Resourceful. I've heard all my life I'm resourceful and, afraid as I am, that's not going to change now. I don't intend to die like this. Any other way would be fine, but not impaled by rocks and left to drown. That's like, I don't know, top three worst ways to die for me? But what else can I do besides plummet?

I look around for some way out of this mess, but there's only one option. Using all my strength, and leg span, I kick off the cliffside in hopes of furthering myself from the rocks...but that's not how falling to your death works, apparently. Instead of moving away from the rocks, I drive myself closer.

I scream and cover my eyes, thinking about my poor mom and dad. If they do find me, I'll be nothing more than a crumpled heap of splattered blood and bone on the rocks. If they don't, well...I'd also rather they don't. I don't want them to spend the rest of their lives dreaming of my corpse among the shale and sea.

I brace for impact. A bright light surrounds me and I sit up, alone in my bed. The gray sheets beneath me look like someone dumped a bucket of water on them. I've never been a night sweater, not to this degree. I'm almost disgusted.

I turn, feeling an ache through my body like I did in fact hit the rocks and a worse one in my head, and see water on the nightstand. Two blue pain pills sit beside it. I brush horribly tangled hair from my eyes and try to remember what happened the night before.

Was it really all just a drunk dream?

●○●○●○●○●○●

Want to see the other endings?
Go back to the start and take another trip through Hellhound's Delight!

SWIM TO SHORE

I *want my mom. I want my dad. I want to go home.*

The shore is farther than the cave and I don't know if I'll make it, but I have to try. I want to try. I need to try, so I do. I force myself to power through the pain that overwhelms me after abandoning the beautiful blue flames and whatever safety their presence promised. I know now that I've made a choice I can't take back. If I stop trying for even a second, the waves will swallow me whole.

A strange feeling grips my heart, squeezing it harder and harder until I'm nearly choking on my own despair as I get closer and closer to the shore. I lose hope of escaping the water's clutches and almost choose to embrace oblivion until my fingers finally find the black sand shore. I claw my way up the coast and collapse, relief washing over me when I'm finally free.

I touch the sand slowly, playing with the grit, before I realize there should be no such shore. Only long stretches of cliff for miles. My journey isn't over yet.

I force myself to stand and face the path ahead, but there is no path. Only a gate, a gate with thick iron bars that siphons away the stress and pain, and fear I've been carrying since I woke up alone.

Someone I recognize, my uncle, stands on the other side of the gate. He looks younger than I've ever seen and stands tall and proud, just as he did before cancer took him. Behind him, far in the distance, I see a magnificent, golden gate. My great-grandparents stand behind it, their arms open while they wait for me.

My heart breaks. How could I do this to my friends and living family? But it passes almost as quickly as it came. I take my uncle's hand and watch him open the gate, leading me to the others who went home before me.

Someday soon, I'll meet my parents at the gates.

And anyone else the hound sends to their doom.

●○●○●○●○●○●

Want to see the other endings?
Go back to the start and take another trip through Hellhound's Delight!

FOLLOW THE LIGHTS

The beautiful blue light calls to me. It whispers my name, begging me to play its game, and I do. I force my freezing arms to move, swimming through terrible waves, pushing closer and closer to the cave until my legs scrape the rocky cave entrance. I don't wince, even as their sharp edges bite the skin under my jeans.

I lift myself from the water, shivering as subterranean air wraps around me, and take the first step inside. My foot makes contact with a patch of moss, and I flinch as the underground world shrouded in darkness comes to life around me.

Colorful skeletal creatures along the cave walls dance as I pass, their glow near blinding. I can feel strength returning as I creep closer to my final destination, my clothes shifting from a water-logged sweater into a dark black robe. I grow warmer (though it might be hypothermia finally setting in) when I step into the single splash of moonlight in the cave's center.

A familiar friend, my hound, brushes against the back of my legs before joining me in the moonlight. It shifts, taking on a new form, bones cracking and popping as it changes like I've changed tonight. It — no, he stands to greet me with a skeletal smile. "It seems I've found myself a worthy replacement."

He holds out his hand and a scythe blossoms from the palm before he turns the handle toward me. It's an invitation and I take it, power coursing through my veins as his body turns to dust with a howling laugh. His job is complete. He can finally find peace.

I balance the scythe in my palm, feeling its weight and its responsibility settle on my shoulders. I know and feel everything in the world, every birth, every death, and every instant in between. I understand my own death, the moment the river claimed me when I drank from its banks, but *before* no longer matters now that I am Death itself.

●○●○●○●○●○●

Want to see the other endings?
Go back to the start and take another trip through Hellhound's Delight!

Don't miss out!

Visit the website below and you can sign up to receive emails whenever JC Ballard publishes a new book. There's no charge and no obligation.

https://books2read.com/r/B-A-XCFH-TYLZ

BOOKS 2 READ

Connecting independent readers to independent writers.

About the Author

J.C. Ballard writes exciting fantasy and contemporary romance novels, featuring bold new worlds, action-packed adventure, and captivating characters. If you let her tell you a story, she promises to pull your heart strings, and leave you aching for adventures beyond your wildest dreams. Born and raised in Oklahoma, this Southern girl has been writing stories for as long as she can remember, often inspired by the people and places around her. When she's not writing, she can often be found in binging her favorite tv shows or curled up with a good book.

Read more at www.jcballard.com.

Milton Keynes UK
Ingram Content Group UK Ltd.
UKHW050208051123
431893UK00025B/621

9 798223 938903